REANIMATED WRITERS PRESS

100 Zombie Bites

An Undead Drabbles Anthology

First edition

ISBN: 978-1-62676-045-5

Contents

Zombie Drabbles

Dear Reader,

Are you ready to read 100 word stories packed with zombies, the undead, zees, walkers, stalkers, ankle-biters, zeds, monsters, crawlers, draggers, rotters, geeks, the risen, stiffs, ghouls, or whatever else you want to call them? No matter their name, one thing is for sure, they are the reanimated dead coming to get the living to feast on their delicious brains! We gave authors 100 words exactly to tell you stories that revolve around zombies and the humans fighting them to survive. We hope you enjoy this carefully selected collection of drabbles, or 100 word stories.

The Reanimated Writers

Wasted Meat by G. Allen Wilbanks

I stared into the pit with disgust. A goat had fallen into my punji trap, but one of the God-damned zombies had stumbled in and attacked the goat. Anything left of the animal now would be too contaminated to eat.

The undead monster stared up at me.

"I see you, too, you bastard."

Wasted meat. Wasted energy. Wasted time.

I returned to the truck to grab my shotgun and a shovel. Nothing to be done except fill in this pit and dig a new one. I cursed my luck. It was going to be another night with an empty belly.

The Awakening by C.A. Verstraete

I opened my eyes and looked around in confusion. Where was I? What happened to me?

The nurse said I'd been sick, I'd been bitten, but they could fix me. They had new medicine.

I tried to understand what she meant. Bitten? By what? Then I remembered… the virus, the panic, the horror when the ill died and returned to life.

I looked down at my pale flesh and back at her normal color. She smiled and readied the shot.

As I watched her, something stirred inside. No medicine would fix what I needed. I grabbed her arm and bit.

Ruckus by Valerie Lioudis

Before, when things were civilized, Ruckus was a shelter dog. He was dropped off for being too BIG, too LOUD, and way too *enthusiastic*. Our family adopted him mere weeks before the first zombie rose.

When our food ran out, Dad threatened to eat him.

Ruckus kept himself out of the stockpot with the first rabbit he brought back home.

We were hungry long before we were running.

When the dead came, Ruckus became the only family member that could keep the rest alive. He had a knack for smelling the corpses.

Once, we saved him. Now, he saves us.

Not This Time by Grivante

The bite burned.

I stared at the oval pattern of ridged teeth marks around my forearm. This was it, all it took. It was over.

From here, I had minutes, maybe an hour, that is if these creatures didn't kill me before I turned.

I thought I'd get away, be lucky, like always. I'd reached in to save her, it was foolish, but I couldn't let her go without trying.

The price for my chivalry burned, throbbing as the infection spread. I only wish she'd lived long enough for me to get to eat her too.

She looked quite delicious.

Rude Interruptions by Eleanor Merry

The zombie hummed lightly as he licked the red delights dribbling from the finger he held, his body vibrating with happiness. Since he woke up, he hadn't been so content, and his belly groaned with approval. The thing beside him groaned too, and he frowned down at its interruption. Picking up the heavy knife beside him, he quickly and surely slid it across the things throat before cutting another finger off and bringing it to his mouth. Closing his eyes, he leaned back into the sun to savor in the warmth of his own being. Today was a good day.

Running by T.D. Ricketts

Running. Keep running and don't stop. Pee on the run. Swing his hammer. Dodge the slow-moving dead.

Grab food, get in and out of houses. Sleep was a luxury.

Avoid cities and population centers. Try to survive on the outskirts.

Running, Keep running, like a Stephen King story.

The dead reached for him. Too close to the city.

The small horde reached for him. Grabbing for the living flesh.

His arms like lead. His legs rubber. His stomach rumbled and growled. His bowels emptied into his shorts.

Moving walking. Don't stop. Just keep moving. So tired.

No safety anywhere.

Chained Melody Hari Navarro

The zombie apocalypse took a shape nobody expected. Though I think secretly we wanted it like this. They aren't contagious, no cravings to eat of our flesh. They don't decay if we feed them. Well maintained they should last a lifetime. They don't horde but they'll follow anywhere. Hence, the collar and chains. They're harmless.

Never had a woman. They sensed things weren't quite right. Least, that's the feeling I got. But this evolution brought my Melody unto me. I keep her in darkness. It's feeding time.

I know she loves me, for every time she sees me she cries.

Tap by A.B. Archambault

Tap.

The noise has been a steady, slow beat for the last hour. Less of a tap, more of a thud, a body hitting the wall.

Tap.

Nothing to worry about. It's just one; can't do much. Might as well go to bed. Handle it in the morning.

Tap.

The stairs creak on the way to the bedroom. It's a comforting sound, normal.

Tap.

They never stop, until they fall apart, or something stops them.

But the living still need to sleep. Lights off, blanket over the head.

Tap.

Its softer now, muffled; deal with it in the morning.

Creak.

Contagion N.M. Brown

An extraordinarily rare system failure unlocked the main control room at one of the largest centers for disease control in the entire United States. Protocol was ignored due to a rush to remedy the situation.

A vial containing the World's deadliest disease fell to the floor; shattering. The disease was airborne... virtually unstoppable.

For the first month, nothing happened.

But soon, the World became rampant with flesh eating organisms; once resembling human beings. Brother turned against brother. Mothers turned on their infants. Food became nonexistent as humanity evolved to only feed on the most organic food of all; flesh.

Nibble by Rissa Blakeley

Numb. Cold. An ache deep within. Addiction niggled his brain. A fuzzy thought. *What happened?*

Stomach twisting in hunger. *Starving.* He groaned, trying to comprehend. A scent grabbed him. Nauseating... No. Heavenly. His mouth watered. Or was that clotted blood sticking to his tongue?

A coppery slap to his senses. The pull to stand and follow the rest of them... Those like him.

So many. Groaning. Grumbling. He spent one second in contemplation, but the hunger ravaging his body felt preternatural, otherworldly.

He stumbled, one foot dragging, an arm dangling. The ache deepened. All he wanted was a taste. Just...one...nibble...

Life? by T.D. Ricketts

After being in the rain and cold he shivered and shook. Finding a dry place that was safe was a priority.

The rain was turning to snow. Nobody knew what the coming winter held for them.

Scattered survivors eked out survival. Groups got eaten, too much noise and attraction for the dead. Hoards overwhelmed them.

He hid and ran all summer long. Hanging on the fringes of suburbia. An old hatchet and a machete his only friends. It was lonely. So lonely.

Sleeping where he could, in trees and on roofs.

What did the future hold? Would life continue?

No Rest for the Obsessed by Beth W. Patterson

You're supposed to be ancient history. You and my husband were through long before I came along.

"There's really not much to tell," he said. "She's crazy . . . not in a fun way, but she won't hurt us."

But you immediately stalked us. Night after night I saw the long curtain of your red hair through my bedroom window. Nobody saw me finally snap, and I had hidden your body far away. Yet here you are, unable to concede. Even in your undead state your corpse still knows where we live. It's my justification for killing you twice.

Old Habits by T.D. Ricketts

Old habits die hard. People die easy. Opening a door and reaching for the light switch. Simple right? But with no power and no lights it did no good. Using the hand that usually held the machete was just stupid. One little mistake.

Banging on the closed door and hearing nothing. Looking in the window and seeing nothing.

No hordes of undead lurking in the area. Just an empty house in the middle of nowhere.

All this meant nothing, just a weeping pus-filled gash on the arm and an inevitable undeath. Not even a bullet to end it. Old Habits.

The Heist by C.A. Verstraete

I knew the old woman never changed her routine on the way to her jewelry store. Same time, same route, every day. Her house looked like an easy hit, too. A dead-end street, no close neighbors. Perfect.

I got in fast, thrilled to find boxes and boxes of fine jewelry. Then everything went wrong—I discovered she'd stayed home sick.

When she reached for the phone, I panicked. Grabbing the heavy instrument, I swung and hit. Blood saturated the blankets. I wrapped her dead body in the sheet and dragged it off the bed.

Minutes later, she began to stir.

God Given Duty by Chloé Harper Gold

Mama told us it was our God-given duty to protect our own. Not ourselves. Our family. That meant that if one of us got infected, it would fall to the others to put them down before the sickness spread and wiped us all out. It's been months since the virus reached Louisiana. We've had to put down my big brother Caleb, my Auntie Jo, and all five of her kids.

My baby sister Lita was bitten three days ago by an infected mosquito. I've been hiding her in the attic. When Mama finds out, she'll put us both down.

Waste by Cassandra Angler

Gnashing teeth and rotting breath. Little girls and their bows, caked in decay. Their mother and father desperate for any other way. They couldn't save them, and now they can't stay. No reason to move forward, no reason to live. Youth and longevity lost to plague. The shotgun barrel harsh in taste, his undead daughters beat against the door. One shot blast and blood pools on the floor. The pounding turns excited, the airs copper scent teasing a meal. Mother steps forward, opening the door. A mothers final act of love, they leave nothing to waste.

Family First by Brandy Bonifas

Joe chambered a round, aiming at the man stealing from his garden.

"Please, I haven't eaten in a while."

Lowering the gun, Joe motioned him inside. "These're my young'uns. Wife's in the cellar preparing for dinner. Reckon we'll feed ya."

"You folks alone? I'm heading to a settlement. You could come."

"We take care of ourselves. Earn your keep. Help my wife carry up some potatoes."

Joe locked the cellar door behind the man, then listened to his screams... and the sound of feeding.

"See kids, I told you we'd take care of your Ma... no matter what. Family first."

Me, You, All of You and I by Joachim Heijndermans

Mmm. Smell that?Of course you do, you beauty. You couldn't, before me. Now you're a good little hunter. All of you are. So much better at this since I began to course through your veins, if a bit more prone to falling apart. You'll be fine without the arm, right?

There they are. Hidden away, behind the wood. But we found them. Break it open. Four of them, all without me. Go ahead, you all. Bite.Rip. Gnash away. Spread me out into more of you.

And there I am, in four new ones of you.

Let's find more.

Teething pains by Zoey Xolton

Carla clapped her hand over her mouth, holding her breath as her heart raced. *She was not alone in the abandoned supermarket.*

Scavenging in the suburbs was akin to a suicide mission…but she'd had no choice. Her little group of survivors were counting on her, children all.

The shuffling drew nearer.

God help me.

Edging quietly down the aisle, she grabbed what she could, shoving it into her knapsack. Peering around shelving, she ventured beyond the displays, her escape route in sight. *Almost there!*

A burning pain, sharp and sudden.

Shock. Confusion. Horror.

An undead child latched onto her leg.

Cry by Cassandra Angler

The sound of a toddler's cry echoes through the streets, there's something off about it. Shrill and airless. I approach from behind. My footsteps catching his attention. His blonde curls bounce as he turns to face me, sniffing air. His face and neck riddled with bite marks. His eyes void of the boy he was supposed to be. Heartbroken I offer him my hand. His toothless gums grind desperately against my fingertips. I offer him the rabbit carcass I have, he coos happily. I raise him to his feet and take his hand.

Dutifully he follows.

Unity by N.M. Brown

The infected were few; small enough in number to be easily contained. No one knew what was to come. Our World was so consumed in superficial battles; it took awhile to notice the spread of disease.

Our Earth became divided; the living against the dead. Humanity finally had a unified perspective. No one hated based on race, religion, political party or sexual preference. Everyone just tried to survive.

All walks and ways of life stood side by side, slaying the undead hand in hand. Peace among the living was finally tangible.

Not that anyone survived long enough to enjoy it.

Original Recipe by Terry Miller

Randy sat in the recliner staring at the white wall. He could feel it, the change. It was so much slower than he anticipated. A few days ago, he gave up sweets. Yesterday, a carrot turned his stomach inside out. The wound on his arm festered, maggots digging through the flesh. Maybe there was still time, he thought.

Randy cut through his arm at the elbow, in desperation, until his forearm separated and fell to the floor. The pain was minimal, surprisingly, but seeing the lifeless limb awoke something deep inside. It wasn't fried chicken, but it was delicious, tender.

Drugs N Brains by Kevin J. Kennedy

I was partying when the zombies attacked. Full of ecstasy and had far too much to drink. It's done something weird. I'm stuck inside. I'm just a brain now. My body controlled and driven by an insatiable hunger. I don't think I'm like the other zombies though. When my victims scream, it sounds like dance music. When I bite into then, the blood tastes like alcohol. Part of me hates what I have become while another part feels like I am on the best, longest, craziest night out ever. Who knew the zombie apocalypse would be such a wild party?

Behold Subject 36 by Umair Mirxa

Abraham plugged another cable into Subject 36, checked all calibrations one last time, and stood back. He felt divine as, at last, he flipped the switch.

"Awaken!" he called imperiously.

Electricity raced through the cables, and coursed through Subject 36. Every piece of equipment in the room exploded.

Twenty minutes later, panicked neighbors found the charred, mangled remains of the eccentric doctor.

A few streets away, Subject 36 licked his fingers, and limped into an alley. Each bite into the doctor's brain had given him a fractured piece of memory.

"I am Abraham," he said, descending upon the stoned beggar.

The Screams by Steve Stred

The screams were what kept me up at night the most.

God, those screams.

The fleeing people would pound on the doors, begging to be let in, but their efforts also brought the hordes. Then they'd scream as they were torn limb from limb, necks attacked by ragged teeth.

I'd found the perfect place to survive until the military regained control. I wasn't about to let anyone take it from me.

But the screams, oh Lord, the screams. They were enough to have me second guess my selfishness.

Maybe it was time to open the doors, let a few in?

The Return by Vonnie Winslow Crist

"Will there be maggots?" asked Maddie.

Aunt Delia nodded.

"Will Jacob recognize me?"

"Draugur know to whom they return and why," answered her aunt.

The door opened.

"Get ready," ordered Delia.

Candlelight illuminated Maddie's husband's rotten, maggoty face.

"You're safe," slurred Jacob. "I bit his head off." He lifted his father's severed head with a decomposing hand.

"Praise be!" exclaimed Delia. "His murderer and your enemy is gone."

"Maddie, if you love me, you must kill me," begged the draugur.

"I cannot," sobbed Maddie.

Rained Out: A City of Devils Story by Justin Robinson

Nothing is as fun as hosing a cop's jalopy down with a tommy-gun. It's a team sport too. The cops might as well have been shooting back with spitballs. I lost a pinkie, half an ear, and looked like Swiss cheese in a nice suit. But I was a zombie. Didn't matter so long as my noggin stayed intact.

A bullet knocked me over. More dropped my pals. The game was over, called on account of lead rain. Time to be arrested. A cop was over me, eclipsing the moon.

"Brains," I told him.

"Sure," he said, cocking his gun.

Outside In by Brandy Bonifas

"Where's my daughter? Who are you?"

"It's me, Mom. Hush now, we have to be quiet." Parting the curtains, I watched as one of the infected shambled across the lawn then bumped repeatedly into the barn.

Taking Mom's dinner tray, I locked her bedroom behind me. I felt bad but couldn't chance her wandering off.

The next morning, I heard soft shuffling and repeated thumps coming from Mom's room. She must be confused again, or maybe...

I sat at the kitchen table, head in my hands, staring at her breakfast tray and debating if I should take it to her.

Snake Head by Chloé Harper Gold

Paul's first job was catching snakes on a golf course. He was supposed to put them in a special box and deliver them to animal control, but sometimes he wouldn't. Instead, he'd kill them in his backyard. He'd cut their heads off and watch their bodies writhe around futilely. He was sixteen.

"Careful, Paulie," his neighbor, Grady, told him. "A snake's head can still bite."

They never did though. Paul was thirty now and a self-appointed zombie-killer. After decapitating his latest mark, he nudged its head with his boot. He regretted it instantly; this one was a biter.

Gazing into the Refrigerator by Veronica Smith

I'm so hungry! I'm digging through my fridge, but nothing looks appetizing. Wait! What's that behind the eggs. Steak? Raw? Ew. That's gross, it's all bloody, it's all ... ooh just look at it. I could cook that up right now. Blood is dripping on the counter as I rip off the plastic. Leaning forward, I lick the blood, savoring it on my tongue. Before I know it, I've eaten the entire steak raw, rubbing a bandage covering a wound I can't remember getting. But it's not enough, not near enough. I hear laughter somewhere in the house. It's dinnertime.

Little White Lies by Kristopher Lioudis

You tell yourself the news has to be wrong. That night, driving home when you hear the first reports.

You tell yourself it will be okay as you move your wife and daughter to the basement a week later when it's in your neighborhood.

You tell yourself you'll fight them off as they crash down the basement steps.

You tell yourself you'll hold on as they try to tear away your little girl.

You tell yourself you can't tell the difference when her screams of terror become screams of pain. The difference is subtle, but it's there.

Easter Parade by Dawn DeBraal

Mary used to make a fashion statement when she was alive. As a zombie, she dressed in old rags. Changes needed to be made. She might be undead, but she still wanted to look her best.

Mary walked down the street, passing up several tasty looking people in search of a fashionable outfit in her size. The woman begged for her life.

"Strip," she told the woman barely remembering how to talk anymore. The woman handed the dress over. Leaving the smelly old rag behind her, Mary had a new step in her shuffle parading the outfit down the street.

The Worst Part by Richard Restucci

He had no sense of time. Had it been a month yet? Maybe. Didn't really matter, this was not something he was going to get better from. The worst part of it was that he always seemed to be hungry.

There was an ear on the road in front of him. He reached up to feel his own ear, but it dropped off when he touched it.

Oh shit! he thought. *What's gonna drop off of me next? A finger? My nose? My...*

He swallowed hard.

No. Please no...

He looked into his pants.

Being hungry wasn't the worst part.

The Offering by Jen Tyes

Heart pounding, I run, dipping and dodging the hands clawing for me. Finally, I find an alley clear of the walking decay. I crouch behind a dumpster, clenching onto the key hanging from my neck. I turn my head to listen for the familiar step and drag of sloshing flesh. *He's coming.* The putrid smell paralyzes me as he slowly makes his way to my hiding place. I see him; blood flows where the key has pierced my skin. Looking down at me, he reaches into his ribcage and presents the remains of his heart. Unable to resist, I feast.

Seeking Safety by Eddie D. Moore

The porch creaked as AJ walked across it. He stepped to the side before knocking just in case someone decided to shoot through the door. A muffled voice inside asked, "What do you want?"

"There's too many biters in the city. I had to get out of there. Can I sleep on your couch tonight?"

"Get off my property!"

"Come on, it's just one night. It's dangerous outside."

The door opened and a female biter with white eyes was shoved outside, teeth snapping.

As AJ ran from the house, he heard the old man shout, "It's dangerous in here too!"

A Mother's Prayer by Andra Dill

Beth never envisioned herself as a murderer but as the virus claimed life after life, she'd become a proficient one. She paced the motel room floor, cradling the motionless babe. An exhausted CNN reporter recited quarantined towns and confirmed government shelters.

No time to reach shelter now.

She glanced at the gore-stained axe. Only a pulverized skull or decapitation would stop the zombies.

Ignoring the pain in her milk-swollen breasts, Beth kissed her daughter's downy head. So tiny. So easily cracked. Tears coursed down her cheeks. One more hour. She prayed the lifeless babe wouldn't rise, and eyed the axe.

A Bite of Inspiration by Umair Mirxa

"Bruce, I do believe this is taking things too far," said Steven. "You are a brilliant writer. You don't have to go to these extremes for inspiration."

"You don't understand, Steven," said Bruce. "I have to see a real one before I ... Steven!"

Bruce screamed as the zombie they'd come looking for appeared behind Steven out of the darkness. Before either of them could move, it had grabbed Steven and bit into his neck.

***

"I'm really sorry, my friend," said Bruce, having shot and killed the zombie. "But now you have been bitten, you'll give me many, many stories."

Last Laugh by Derek Dunn

October was Stanley's favorite month. Haunted attractions were opening all over town. He'd already been to the haunted hospital twice. Tonight, he'd invited Beth. He laughed as she jumped at all the predicted scares.

As they entered the zombie corridor, something seemed off. The spooks looked so real. Either they'd had vast improvements in their makeup, or their flesh was actually rotting. Their behavior was different, too. Stanley squeezed past as fast as he could, but one grabbed him. Beth laughed as the tide had turned, but screams soon took over as the zombie dug sharp incisors into his jugular.

Dead and Rotting by Wondra Vanian

Finding an unlocked apartment in the city was easy enough. Finding one safe enough to take shelter in was harder.

"Your turn," Rosie said, adjusting her makeshift armor.

"Fine. Cover me."

Nudging the door open with his foot, Dorian raised his gun. He choked back bile when the smell hit him.

Unfortunately, dead and rotting didn't mean safe. A few steps into the apartment proved just *how* unsafe.

Dorian heard the shuffle seconds before Rosie's warning shout. Turning, he fired without hesitation.

"Daddy?" A girl cried from the adjoining room.

Rosie gasped.

Dammit.

He'd forgotten... stench didn't always mean zombie.

Served Cold by Robin Braid

I stood in the darkened garden and gazed through the window. He was there with the family, the warm glow from the fireplace illuminated their faces, happy and content. A little girl ran to him and he put his hands under her arms and lifted her onto his lap. Those hands that had closed around my throat.

I made my way to the backdoor, leaving a trail of mud in my wake. Clods of dirt dropped from my hands as a pulsating red river rushed a gnawing hunger through me. I shuffled inside and closed the door. Home again brother.

Playing God by Amber M. Simpson

"It's working!" Dr. Michaels cried, pulling the empty syringe from the dead girl's neck. His intern, Lucy, chewed her lower lip. She wasn't exactly sure what the syringe consisted of, the substance a thick, yellowish-green with flecks of floating matter. But it was now in the dead girl's body, fingers twitching at her sides, eyelids fluttering open.

For months, Dr. Michaels had tried to reanimate the dead, and it seemed he'd finally succeeded, with Lucy his reluctant accomplice. But as the not-so-dead-girl shot up from the table and bit into Dr. Michaels' face, Lucy knew they'd made a terrible mistake.

Bare Hands by Rich Rurshell

"I'll have another go bare hands. Let another one in, Rich,"
shouted Terry.

Dan and I opened the pub door, revealing the ocean of undead
in the street outside. I dragged in the closest one, a man in work
boots, shorts and a Hi-Viz, and Dan slammed the door shut
again, locking it.

The undead guy tried to bite us, but bounced harmlessly off our
bite-proof suits. We pushed him into the middle of the room
towards Terry, who stood with his fists raised, bare-chested,
grinning like a lunatic.

I'm not sure who scared me more, Terry or the undead.

Bloody Vengeance by Charlotte O'Farrell

The dead began to rise – but only some of them. Only the murder victims.

They hunted their killers without mercy. Though they had vacant eyes, drooling mouths and rotting flesh, their commitment to their task never wavered.

Once they had destroyed the people who killed them, they left their bitten remains behind. But they too rose, now the victims of murder themselves.

All of the people killed in the crossfire as the undead sought their revenge awoke, hungry for flesh and justice.

Soon, the world was overrun with zombie factions, fighting each other in an endless war of the dead.

The Cure Rich by Richard Restucci

She stared at it in the waning light. She had cupped her hand around the wound attempting to stem the blood. A futile gesture, she knew. It hurt, but not nearly as badly as she had thought it would. The real pain would begin in a few hours, then it would consume her.

Salty tears flowed freely. Not because of what was about to happen, but because she had thought of her family, long since dead.

I'm coming, she thought to them.

Her revolver sat in front of her. Remorseless, like the slavering things outside.

Moonlight gleamed off the chrome.

Beware of Zombie by G. Allen Wilbanks

Mike wandered over to his neighbor's house and found Alex nailing a sign to his gate.

"Beware of zombie? You're kidding."

Mike heard a low moan coming from the backyard and realized it was no joke. "Why not get another dog?" he asked.

"Zombies are easier. You don't have to feed them, walk them, or pick up after them. And you can't make friends with it by throwing food over the fence."

"That's crazy," Mike muttered.

Alex shrugged. "Maybe. But while we're on the subject, next time you want to borrow any of my tools, you should probably ask first."

Don't Mask Don't Tell by Beth W. Patterson

Nobody knows when she truly died, for the picture perfect mask she wore had fooled everyone.

It probably began when the light within her began to dim and the clay veneer of makeup got brighter daily. Her tongue thickened with unspoken forbidden words. She lost interest in her friends, music, and even food. Silent, thin, and wearing a painted smile, she was deemed the perfect wife. No one heard her whisper about brains.

One night she finally ripped off her mask, peeling away her entire face. As soon as she lunged for her sleeping husband's skull, she regained her appetite.

Digger by Brian Rosenberger

Lulu was a good dog, came when called, never begged for food, and only barked at strangers and cats.

Lulu was a pure-bred, long-haired Dachshund. Beautiful. A lap dog. She never met a lap she didn't like. She was a kisser, a licker, her tail always wagging.

She was also a digger.

Dachshunds were bred to hunt badgers. The cute wiener dog, with razor-sharp teeth and claws, could be an underground assassin.

I cried like a little girl when Lulu died. Buried in the backyard Lulu loved.

I wasn't surprised to see her, dirty, tail wagging.

Lulu was a digger.

They Are Coming by Cindar Harrell

The sound of my heavy breathing filled the confined space, creating a deafening roar in tandem with the blood rushing in my head. I had escaped, but barely. My husband wasn't so lucky.

I clenched the flashlight he had handed me like a lifeline, although I knew it wouldn't save me. They had no fear of light. They had no fear at all.

"Just calm down," I whispered, trying to control my rapid heart rate. I was safe in here.

The sound of dull scratches on wood pierced through the haze in my mind.

It's over now. They are coming.

Captive Audience by Joel R. Hunt

Nicola had waited her whole life for this chance, and she wasn't about to waste it. All eyes in the crowded theater were on her; the center of attention.

She didn't disappoint. Her fingers caressed the harp like a lover, dancing along its strings and drawing out notes of perfection.

Throughout the auditorium, the crowd writhed in their seats, desperately trying to break free. Rotting skin tensed against rope. Hungry jaws bit down on gags. A hundred bloodshot eyes watched, locked onto the living flesh on stage.

"What's that?" Nicola asked them, "You'd like an encore? Well, if you insist."

Office Party by Derek Dunn

The office was dead. Even for a Friday afternoon, the place seemed eerily quiet. Doug packed his briefcase and headed to the men's room before clocking out.

Someone moaned in the adjacent stall. Doug ignored the crude wails and continued his business. He flushed the toilet and slipped as he stood. Catching himself on the handicap rail, Doug looked down. A stream of blood had seeped from under the wall. He rushed out, not bothering to check on the man.

The office was alive now, though his co-workers didn't look it. With outstretched bloodied arms, they charged him in unison.

Farm Hand by N.M. Brown

The growling grows distant. After running for miles, I'm finally making some headway.

Before the change started, I used to drive by an abandoned barn on my way to work. I pray it's empty and that I can hide out here from the undead.

The field is still and silent. It doesn't look like anyone's here. I crawl through the rows of vegetation, stopping to rest at the old scarecrow's post.

Something twitches above my head, almost indiscernible at first. Arms that should have been straw made thrash violently. The Scarecrow's face contorts into a snarl.

I am not alone.

Tasty Treats by Brian Rosenberger

This wasn't Luke's regular route. He was lost. The middle of nowhere. Subdivision after subdivision. They all looked the same at this point.

The stereo in the Ice Cream Truck was dead, had been for days.

Still they came. The children. Their parents. They all came to see the Ice Cream Man.

The ice cream and other frozen novelties had either melted or been consumed by Luke. The sugar rush kept him awake, kept him alert, kept him alive.

The Ice Cream Truck was low on gas.

Still they came. The dead children, hungry for tasty treats, hungry for Luke.

Love in Life and Undeath by Nerisha Kemraj

Low guttural moans stemming from the undead bodies filled the somber night. Jason and Lydia ran through the street as the horde drew closer. They entered the last house on the street and bolted the door. Jason hurried to board up broken window.

The stench reached Lydia before she heard its groan. Screaming as teeth sank into her leg, she ran towards the window's light, falling into Jason's arms.

"It got me," she said, hopeless tears filling her eyes.

"It's ok," he said.

"Go. Save yourself." Her last words before convulsing.

Grief-stricken, he held her, waiting for her to turn.

The Dare by Steve Stred

It was just a stupid dare and now I was paying for it.

"My dad says you can eat their flesh. You won't turn cuz they didn't bite you."

Bryan sounded confident if not scared.

"I double-dog dare you," I said then, knowing he wouldn't.

He popped his switch blade open and cut off a small square from the dead man's shoulder, even as it gnashed and thrashed. We'd ripped off its lower half already, so it wasn't a threat.

Before I could stop him – in his mouth it went. Two chews and then a swallow.

Then he started frothing.

I Am Virus by Veronica Smith

I awake inside a new host, remembering the last one was nothing but a cold shell; eating any living thing in its path. But this host is different. It's warm and alive; scared but full of life. I spread all my tiny little arms and legs until I'm everywhere; blood, organs, skin. I like this new home and plan to settle here for a while. Unfortunately, as time goes on, it's condition declines until it's almost the same as my previous host. This one isn't as decayed but it's getting there fast. It is time to find a new home.

The Plan by Stuart Conover

Jasper looked through the window for the twentieth time.

Maresol should be there already.

He knew the plan was to keep moving.

Lovers or not, she would have left.

She always followed the plan.

Swearing, he opened the concealed door.

Maresol would kill him if she wasn't dead.

Sneaking back a few he came across five zombies.

They were feasting on fresh prey.

Thankfully, it wasn't Maresol.

He could see her.

Hiding.

Just past the undead.

They'd see her when they stood.

Only one of them would make it out alive.

"I love you" he shouted and began to run.

Breakfast Craving by Shawn M. Klimek

Rory awoke craving human flesh. This was new. Her usual breakfast was black coffee with cornflakes and milk. Yet this morning…no, wait. Not morning. The sun was too high. Painfully bright. Nor was this her bed. The mattress was asphalt. She seemed to have awoken in the street. But how? She ached everywhere. Her muscles felt stiff, slow and yet, *such strength!* This hunger drove every muscle relentlessly. Human flesh! She could smell it near. That man. Huddling two daughters. *Damn. Moving too fast.* What about that one with the baseball bat, approaching tantalizingly near? *Come closer, fool!* she thought.

Cradle to Grave by Chloé Harper Gold

Trish and Marla had talked about this countless times, but always under the assumption that the scenario was hypothetical. They had been best friends for their entire lives. From cradle to grave. Neither wanted to live in a world that didn't have the other.

But their imagined scenario wasn't hypothetical anymore.

"You ready?" Trish asked around a throat coated with pus. She looked into Marla's eyes, yellowed, bloodshot, and crusted with infection. They matched her own.

"Yeah," Marla said softly. "I love you."

"I love you, too."

They held their guns to each other's heads and left the world together.

Noticed by Belinda Brady

I keep my distance as I walk behind my target, ducking out of sight whenever he turns around. He's walking alone, not noticing anything or anyone around him.

How times change.

At school, he noticed everything and everyone – especially me. He bullied me daily, not stopping until graduation. How I longed to be unnoticed.

He stops suddenly, growling at something on the road. I sneak up behind him and stab his skull with my knife. He collapses in a heap and I lean over him, smiling as my zombie tormentor perishes.

Now he knows what it's like to be noticed.

Nibble #2 by Rissa Blakeley

Lips cracked, oozing. The foreign taste lingered. Not like the candy she loved. Darker. It plucked, buzzed. Something awoke. She struggled to move.

Twisting around, she remembered. *Daddy?* Her hip cracked, knee buckled.

Tumbling... A small pile of limbs and rotting flesh. She turned her gaze, something familiar catching her attention.

Sunny. The dingy, red-stained bear. A button loose. A pink lollipop matted in its fur. A pungent scent thwarted her attention.

Death tickled her brain. Looking, she scraped her cheek on the pavement. Layers torn away, exposing raw, rotten flesh.

A man stumbled past. She grumbled, "Daddy... Nigh' night..."

Dead & Buried by Joel R. Hunt

Being a cemetery caretaker was lonely work. Martin often heard voices carried to him on the wind, only to find that no-one was there. This time, though, it wasn't his imagination.

Plot 153f – the most recent interment in the graveyard – was calling out to him. He heard the young lady's scratches and moans beneath the fresh soil.

She'd been buried alive.

"Don't panic," Martin shouted into the ground, "I'll get my shovel, hold on!"

He set off at a sprint to his toolshed, but faltered along the path.

The same groaning noises were coming from every plot in the cemetery.

The Human Holocaust by Grivante

It's teeth shivered, porcelain daggers anxious for my flesh.

They'd pursued us up twenty flights, into the high-rollers quarters.

Where the other half lived.

But here, now, the living were outnumbered by these creatures, the dead.

They'd come from the sewers, the lowest of the low, eating through the layers of society, not caring about social order.

Only feeding their hunger, just as we had.

Throughout the universe, they called us the Devourer of Worlds.

Planet Hoppers.

Planet Destroyers.

The Human Holocaust.

We were feared by planets like we feared these undead beasts.

This planet had decided to fight back.

Survivors Can't Be Choosers by Wondra Vanian

They took an indirect route through the village, sticking to the shadows. Freddy rolled across alleys and crouched behind abandoned vehicles. The apocalypse hadn't taught him a lick of discipline.

Lana followed more cautiously. God, she missed the days when there were enough people left to pick your friends.

A face appeared in a broken window, startling Lana.

"Don't go that way," the bedraggled woman warned. "There are zombies."

Lana opened her mouth to warn Freddy, yards ahead, then closed it again.

What'd'ya know? she thought, climbing through the window with the help of her new friend. She *could* choose.

Zombie Love by Dawn DeBraal

When Freddie tried to hug Rita, his arm fell off. He was very sad as he looked at the appendage that lay on the ground. Lately, everything that was attached to his body was falling off. He picked up his lost arm with his good one, popping it back in place. With pursed lips he went in, to kiss Rita. This time his jaw fell off clattering to the floor. Rita picked up his jawbone, snapping it back onto his skull. Freddie was anxious about anything else that could fall off, so they decided to keep things between them platonic.

The Musician by Tina Merry

As dawn came, the sky turned dusty pink. She crept quietly out, terrified of what she'd find. Hiding for weeks, she'd exhausted all resources and had no choice but leave her sanctuary, desperate for food. Haunting strains of beautiful music drew her to a house, and she peered inside. She couldn't make sense of what she saw: a zombie, dressed in a tuxedo, covered in blood and at the piano, playing Fur Elise. Suddenly she smiled. If this is what the world was becoming, and a zombie could still make such beautiful music, perhaps everything was going to be OK.

The Meaningful Choice by Russell Hemmell

Sonora Island, Jurassic attraction park.

A morning like any other, except for the strange, electricity-charged storm that forced the whole facility to shut down for the day. It opened again the morning after, together with the Hell's gates.

Screams, puddles of blood, severed limbs scattered on the ground.

The visitors expected the cloned allosaurus to be alive, not undead; the pterodactyl to soar in the sky, not out of the disposal site.

When the dinosaurs broke the fences shambling forward like an army of darkness, there was just time for one Leica shot or a prayer. Both tokens for eternity.

The End and the Beginning by Jessica Gomez

My brothers body is lowered into the frozen ground, hitting home that I failed as his protector. The crisp air causes my breath to fog in front of me with each exhale, as guilt weighs heavily, despair the main ingredient. The ability to cry was stolen when death permanently embedded itself behind my retinas after the worlds downfall. Only a second passes and the decision is made, my time on this earth is dwindling. Raising the gun against my temple, I keep my eyes fixed, and pull the trigger. The barrel slams, but nothing happens. Not even God wants me.

Tested on Animals by Jacek Wilkos

The test phase of a new biological weapon looks promising. A cat has been infected with the virus through droplets. After eight hours the object died. Ten minutes later an autogenic reanimation occurred. Post mortem state of the animal is stable. Before our undead pet is still a series of tests, including adaptability, electroencephalography, computed tomography, stimulus–responses, completed with vivisection, craniotomy and open brain study.

We both Erwin and I are very excited. For a week we will "own" an unusual pet – a zombie cat.

– How shall we call him? – Erwin asked.

The answer is obvious to me.

– Schrödinger.

Island of Zombies by Cecelia Hopkins-Drewer

Everyone in the lifeboat cheered when they saw land.

"We are saved!"

We dragged the boat up onto the shore and looked around nervously. The inhabitants appeared friendly as they came forward to greet us.

Eyes dull, hands reaching, mouth salivating.

"What happened here?"

This was no indigenous population, but a collection of zombies.

"Run."

"Hide!"

"Stay together."

We pressed further onto the island, unwittingly progressing towards the source of the infection. An abandoned village.

One pesky zombie woman was loitering near the well. She almost seemed capable of intelligible speech.

"Don't dr...."

We clubbed her. The village was ours.

I See You by D.M. Burdett

There's a smell in the air I can't ignore; it dances on the wind, caresses my senses.

My body tenses. I stop to listen.

Then I see her.

A small child stumbles out of the undergrowth and into the clearing. Ragged clothes hang off her too-skinny frame. Dark circles ring wild eyes, and wet crimson colours her once innocent face.

Moonlight illuminates her graceless fall as she collapses to the ground only steps away, landing with a grunt.

Then she sees me.

But the white-hot compulsion has already enveloped me in its warmth.

She closes her eyes; accepts her fate.

Worse Than a Zombie Bite by Hayley Lawson

I wish he'd been bitten.

The evening rain battered down on the windowpane, as Ethel's husband, Jeff, groaned out in pain.

Ethel peaked her head around the kitchen door, Jeff laid out on the sofa. His mouth draped downwards, making an upside-down smile. *If only we could laugh again.*

"I'm dying," Jeff replied with a heavy sigh.

"Yes, my dear, you're dying. You have the dreaded Man Flu. A virus worse than and zombie bite. That brings fear to woman all around the world." *I could let a zombie in, then I'd end my misery.*

Ethel headed to the door …

And the Winner is... by G.B. Burgess

I sprinted down the street.

The zombies' feet thudded right behind me, like the budda budda budda of drums before the announcement of a prize winner. And there were only two possible winners; me or the hoard.

If the zombies won, their prize would be my flesh. Hot, moist, tangy with panic.

If I was the victor, I'd be rewarded with the boarded-up house at the end of the street, and a chance to live another day in this wreckage of a world.

Another day of fear, loneliness and hopelessness.

I ran on, half hoping the zombies would catch me.

Today is the first day of the rest of your life by C.S. Anderson

The dead only attack the sad.

That fact has been established and has formed the basis of survival in our little post-apocalyptic corner of the world.

Put on a happy face.

Inspirational posters cover all the walls and solar powered flat screens broadcast old three stooges and Abbot and Costello routines.

Who's on first? Laugh you bastards.

A woman starts to sob and the hordes outside cock an ear and prepare to attack.

The guards put a knife to her throat.

Put on a happy face.

Nibble #3 by Rissa Blakeley

Gasping, she woke, instincts on fire. "Luna!"

They'd crashed into a light pole. Bodies everywhere, including her daughter and husband. Trapped, legs numb, pinned under the dash and unable to move.

"Noah! Help!" she sobbed.

Monsters roamed the streets. They fled, and she had failed them.

Rumbles. Grunts. She looked through the spiderwebbed windshield. "Monsters... Noah! Luna!"

Turning to the driver's side window, she gasped. Her young daughter staggered to standing and picked up Sunny. It was enough to see the gruesome facial injury. "Nonono..."

Blood... And the monsters swarmed, the end near.

Eyes closed, she waited for the blackness.

Home Alone by Scott Deegan

Dad was supposed to be home, he promised he would be home at seven. At eight twenty, Tammy checked the street and saw Billy the neighbor kid walking in circles. Billy had been going in circles ever since his mom chewed his right leg off from mid calf down. Tammy had to admit that it was funny watching a zombie walk in circles because one leg was shorter than the other. It was also sad, she had been Billy's babysitter.

Hearing the back door open, Tammy ran to the kitchen. Dad fell into the house and the zombie horde followed.

All the World's a Shipwreck by Harrison Herz

All the world's a shipwreck,
   Its hull breached by a virulent virus,
   And all the uninfected men and women merely flotsam.
   They have their lives and then their undeaths.
   And one man, in his time, plays many parts.
   At first the infant, mewling from malnutrition. Their loud
cries that must be stifled, even unto death;
   And then the school-boy, creeping to avoid zombies.
   And then the scavenger, seeking provisions to postpone the
inevitable.
   Then a soldier, aiming for the headshot.
   And then at last, the elderly. So rare, so few in number,
   Sans teeth, sans eyes, sans hair, sans everything.

Payment of Debt by Donna Marie West

"The brute beat me almost daily," I said. "I want him to pay; death is too good for him."

The *bokor* sold me his unholy elixir and told me what it would do.

I put it in my husband's soup.

"Tastes like crap," he said, his usual complaint. He ate it all.

That evening he fell sick. Soon he was paralyzed and turning blue. I called the *bokor* to come for him.

The day after his burial, my husband returned, blank-eyed and dumb, smelling of the grave. A shell of the man he'd been.

Now he would pay his debts.

I'm in Hell by Brandy Yassa

I dreamed I died. I open my eyes and am hit with such a powerful wave of pain and hunger, I can do nothing but moan in anguish. My guts cramp with emptiness and cold, and I am compelled to search for a source of warmth and sustenance.

Then… a scent and a promise of relief.

What little thought there is, is obliterated in a wash of warm red and a frenzy of gnashing teeth and grasping , digging fingers.

Too quickly the scent has faded and the warmth cooled.

I must find the scent of warm, red deliverance again.

Decisions by Brett Nikirk

It happened so fast. The neighbour lady wandered in from the street. The next thing I know she was on top of him. I screamed and tore my son away from her. Locking the door, I left my boy sitting in the kitchen. His eyes were beginning to fog. I grabbed my gun and went to the washroom for our first aid kit but it was too late. I already hear his banging and moaning on the other side of the door. My poor baby. Only one bullet to the brain will end this. Whether it's his or my own.

Sate the Hunger by Lee Franklin

Violent energy swirls in the air as the crowd grows. Gulping air, it reeks of food, and fear. My limbs are chained, each one to a pick-up. Hunger burns my stomach like acid. My body screams, demanding to be fed. There is no fear, just the agonising tear of hunger. The throbbing engines accelerate into a roar. I taste dust as my limbs are plucked from my body. My leg twitches in the dirt as they cheer. My jaws shudder, snapping as the food steps closer; taunting, torturing me. The axe bites into my skull, the hunger is finally sated.

The Zombie's Revenge by Delaney McCormick

As rain pounded the streets of the French Quarter, Isabella heard the thunder as the tombs began to creek open. The curse had worked.

Reanimated corpses moved in unison, their elegant burial clothing now tattered and hanging like rags on their gaunt frames. Following Isabella down Decatur Street they staggered, becoming more ravenous with every step.

Throwing open the door to Brisbane's shop, Isabella smiled wickedly as fear overtook the loathsome man. "Zombies, feed!" she ordered, as her undead warriors ripped the flesh from his bones, blood running in rivulets down their pale chins. Never enrage a voodoo queen.

The Hordes by Chris Bannor

Everything he'd worked so hard to build was destroyed; gone in a single sweep of a mindless horde. It had taken years to secure the encampment and find people he could trust. For five years everything had run as smoothly could be expected with flesh-eating monsters handmade in a lab ravaging the land.

Everything changed two days ago though. The horde ripped through the walls and shredded everything; food, security, and the people he had come to call family.

He could survive the zombies.He could survive the end of civilization. It was the damn human hordes that he hated.

Dammit by Jae Mazer

The meal scrambled away, his living, juicy calves flexing as he escaped Shelia's skeletal grasp.

"Want meat," Shelia groaned.

Shelia lunged forward. But there was no lunging, just a squelching slither as her arms heaved her carcass across the ground. The meal exhaled, the horror draining from its face, replaced by relief.

Creaks and cracks sang out as Sheila twisted her neck to examine the remains of her body.

But it wasn't there.

The lower half of Sheila was several meters away, rotted off at the ribs, ichor oozing from the flaps of skin sloughing off her chest.

"Dammit Sheila."

Turn by B.J. Tunnell

I gasp as I peel back the dressing from the bite wound on my leg. It's ghastly and strips of flesh pull away with it, stuck to the bandage as I check beneath. It's been two days since I fought them off. Two days since I lost Tristan. There were just too many. I couldn't save him. I barely saved myself. My head is pounding and I can feel the heat radiating from my body. My stomach churns and growls. Smells are so much…more, overwhelming my senses. My mouth waters. My hunger grows. I can think of nothing else.

Helpless by Dean M. King

My God, what's happened? The man who stumbled into her had been covered in blood; there was no mistaking its coppery odor. People were stampeding by, crying, moaning. There were explosions, tinkling glass. *Another terrorist attack?* Melissa got down on her knees and groped around for her white cane. Someone tripped over her and went down on the concrete with a grunt. She could hear others coming, moving slower, wet breathing sounds. *Walking wounded?* Thank God, a hand on her arm. Someone stooping to help. *Wait, oh, God! Pain!* Teeth sinking into her face, into her skull. Others pile on.

Funeral Crasher by Amber M. Simpson

My eyes snapped open. A man's voice droned, a woman sobbed. I raised to sitting, joints cracking like twigs. Gasps filled the air. I was inside a casket, in a funeral parlor.

What the hell? I said. "Wuuuh uh huuu?"

Someone screamed.

"Charlotte?"

I blinked at the vaguely familiar man.

"Oh, baby," he cried, embracing me. He smelled delicious.

My body surged with want, with *need*. Holding him tight, I bit his neck, tearing off flesh; ripping out tendons. Screams bounced off the walls as he jerked in my arms, his savory juices filling my mouth.

Yum, I said. "Yuuuuhh."

Through the Streets by Melissa Algood

She'd been chasing me for hours, yet felt longer.

I let my schoolbooks fall to the ground once we made eye contact, and ran. There was no final destination for me, only my Vans hitting the pavement like a hammer away from her. Incessant growling, shuffling, and a snapping jaw tailed me on the city streets.

I couldn't go on forever, therefore after a few hours, I turned and stared at her. Eyes bloodshot, red-tinted drool dripping from the side of her mouth, hands coated in crimson. Helpless without a weapon, I cried as she ravaged me, "Please don't, Mommy."

Gnatha's Congregation by Anthony Giordano

"Just my fucking luck!"

"Shut the fuck up, Frank!"

Frank was right, though. After the asteroid; the dead rose, the living turned. Blank-eyed shamblers consumed, without rhyme or reason.

Our egress brought us here; a compound of lunatics, worshippers of an esoteric arachnid god.

Laughable Halloween-store cloaks, spider face paint. But their guns were all business.

A rough altar. A comedic cleric, sharpening fang-shaped blades. A large bowl, plates.

I see shuffling zombies past the chain link fence, denied their feast. I see Frank, dragged to the altar.

"Just my fucking luck!" he moans again. "I'm still gonna get eaten!"

Livestock by Joseph Easterly

"I'll take number 16."

Daddy handed a bunch of money to the ugly salesman. They shook hands.

On the way home, Mommy and Daddy talked about the green man in the back of the truck. He was chained down, but I think he was dancing. I'll bet he was smiling under his black hood.

"Rebuild the fence."

"Till the field."

I asked why the silly man had the same flower on his arm as Uncle Jimmy.

"He...it does not, Ellie!"

Daddy made a tight smile. His face shook and a tear fell down his cheek.

He continued.

"Plug the well."

Another Option by A.S. Charly

One step… another… so hungry… lumbering down Main Street. The wind rushes… through desolate skyscrapers… blows dust in my face. There are others… stumbling around. Empty faces… until… a scream.

Movement… must hurry. That sweet iron smell…. A crowd forms… loud noises… and more screams. Exciting… there's food!

Can't get through… too much competition… a shoving mass. Someone pumps into me… my arm falls off.

I stare at it… greenish skin… a few maggots squirming. Unbelieving… no pain… no emotions… nothing.

The squealing has ceased…. My stomach growls… in disappointment.

I reach for my detached limb… and take a bite.

Not Going to Make It by Richard Restucci

She was tired from all the running and terror. Probably why she hadn't seen it stumble into the road. She had jerked the wheel hard to the right and suddenly they were airborne, flipping over and over.

She awoke to an upside-down world. Hanging from her seatbelt, she blinked, trying to fathom what had happened. A growl from her right drew her attention. Her husband also hung from his seatbelt. She fought him as he frantically ripped the air trying to get to her.

Footsteps scraped the pavement outside. She screamed when a bloody hand reached through her broken window.

Nice People by A.B. Archambault

Jerry was happy as they ambled down the street. One of a hundred in the group, out for a stroll. He had never had this many friends. It felt good to belong.

There was a girl he had been watching; with a springy step, especially considering the twisted leg. Maybe he would talk to her. And the guy in front of him, was so cool. You almost didn't notice the holes in his shirt, or the bit of entrails sticking out. He could learn from someone like him.

Yes, everyone got along so well. They even had a chant. Braaaaiiins.

A Night to Remember by Gabriella Balcom

"You barely know Jeb," Cathy protested. "Only a weirdo would wanna meet in an abandoned cemetery."

Vera shrugged. "He promised me a Halloween night to remember."

"I *loved* the seance," she told him later. "And, your scary stories had me thinking I heard stuff."

Jeb's nose fell off when he grinned.

"Your makeup's great!" she exclaimed.

Patting his face, Vera snickered when his skin sloughed off at her touch. The blood dripping from his flesh seemed so lifelike. Smelled real, too.

Realizing it *was,* she turned to flee.

More zombies appeared around her, closing in.

The Race by Valerie Lioudis

Fifty thousand dollars would get Sheila's family out of Zone D, and into Zone C. She might even be able to get a fixer upper in Zone B if they were willing to stack like cordwood in the bedrooms. Every zone was that much further from the living dead.

All Shelia needed to do was outrun the other contestants. Well, outrun or push into the horde. Either way would work. All that was required was to be the last one standing. The cameras fed the race into every home in New Utopia.

Where entertainment was just a foot race away.

Curse Your Creations by Umair Mirxa

Cassandra summoned a word of power, let it course through her, and then flow outward. Invisible, it rippled away from her, and ripped through the horde of zombies. Heads rolled, guts spilled, and limbs flew across the village square.

"No!" shrieked Shawn, running in behind the horde, and narrowly surviving the spell. "No, no, no! What have you done to my beautiful creations?"

"Your creations?" said Cassandra, staring at him in disbelief. "You created these accursed monstrosities?"

"Well, of course I did. Spent years perfecting them too!

Shawn gagged, coughing up blood, and disintegrated under the force of Cassandra's curse.

Bugged by Dawn DeBraal

If it weren't for the car, he'd have been alright. Dennis didn't know how long a zombie could live. He was doing fine until the Volkswagon hit him. He was messed up. Dennis was able to fix his leg using a couple of boards tied with rope. It wasn't the best, but it kept him upright. He knew that in his former life, he would have been howling in pain. Dennis tried his first few steps, happy that he could walk again. He was going to find that little beetle and crush it, along with the guy who was driving.

Childhood Delights by Eleanor Merry

Cassie giggled as she skipped away from the still warm corpse. Even in her new form, the idea of art and creation thrilled her. After coming upon the wounded man, she frowned at the state he was in. Ignoring his moans for help, she began to make him 'pretty' again, using various implements in the surrounding forest. Stepping back to survey her work, she applauded herself for the use of greens and how well it complimented the vivid reds. *How festive*, she thought to herself. Singing lightly under her breath, she left the forest in search of her next project

Flying Fists of the Undead by Robin Braid

They couldn't get me. Hands clawed the air, teeth gnashed, but I slipped out of range and struck back. Hard fists smashed through soft, decaying flesh. Bodies fell but others clambered over them, it was relentless. I dropped and swept my leg around, bones snapped as more hit the ground. If I could clear a path, I'd break for the shelter of the woods.

I rolled backwards and I was out, into the air, falling. The river was far below. I closed my eyes. I wasn't sure I would make it, but they didn't get me. They didn't get me.

Lend Me Your Arms by Harrison Herz

Friends, family, neighbors, lend me your arms;
   We come to re-bury the dead, not to raise them.
   The evil that men do lives after them;
   The good is oft lost when their brains are eaten;
   As it is sadly with those here. Our noble mayor
   Hath told you zombies were ravenous:
   If it were so, it was a grievous fault,
   And grievously hath the townsfolk answer'd it.
   So began they all, all honourable people–
   Before they lost their reason. Bear with me;
   My heart is in the coffins there,
   And I must pause till it come back to me.

Gunman by Brett Nikirk

I dragged his feet towards the unmarked grave. Looking at the hole, he must have clawed away for days before pushing through the topsoil. I buried the fool after he tried to fight back when I was robbing him. Two weeks later he came slumping into the saloon, his rotting bare chest showing five oozing bullet holes. He moaned and reached out for me when I placed my revolver against his temple and fired. I tied his corpse to the back of my horse and left town quickly. This is the first man I have ever needed to bury twice.

Links

We hope you enjoyed this collection of zombie drabbles. If you are so inclined, we would love it if you left an honest review on Amazon, GoodReads, or BookBub. To find out more about The Reanimated Writers, please join us in our Facebook Fan Group, or pop over to our website ReanimatedWriters.com to learn more about our group and the authors in it.

For More Zombie Stories check out The Undead Worlds Series

CPSIA information can be obtained
at www.ICGtesting.com
Printed in the USA
LVHW110840111119
636959LV00009B/3479/P